Waldo the Giant has fallen madly in love with a picture of the Princess. Heavy Hetty, Waldo's next-door-neighbour tries to talk Waldo out of it:

"She's too small. Couldn't wrestle for toffee. Probably only comes up to your knee."

"So?" replied Waldo, "Love conquers all."

But when Waldo actually gets to meet the Princess it is not at all as he expected and he learns a valuable lesson.

A charming, witty, heart-warming tale by the popular Kaye Umansky.

OTHER BOOKS BY KAYE UMANSKY

Kaye Umansky

The Romantic Giant

Illustrated by Doffy Weir

Barn Owl Books

The Romantic Giant was first published by Hamish Hamilton in 1994

This edition first published in 2003 by Barn Owl Books
157 Fortis Green Road, London N10 3LX
Barn Owl Books are distributed by Frances Lincoln,
4 Torriano Mews, Torriano Avenue, London NW5 2RZ

ISBN 1-903015-25-1

Designed and typeset by Douglas Martin
Printed and bound in China by Imago

Waldo the giant was in love. His dream girl was the beautiful princess Clarissa, who lived in the palace down in the valley and whose picture he had seen in a magazine. She had golden curls, periwinkle blue eyes and a cute little upturned nose which made Waldo go weak at the knees.

He showed the picture to Heavy Hetty, his next-door neighbour.

Heavy Hetty was a wrestler. She didn't say much, but her biceps were amazing.

"Look!' he said. "Look at the hair! Look at the eyes! Look at that nose! Isn't she beautiful?"

Hetty put down the rock she was squeezing and looked.

"Too small," she grunted. "Couldn't wrestle for toffee. Probably only comes up to your knee."

"So?" said Waldo. "Love conquers all. I'm going to marry her and bring her to live up here."

"She's used to a palace. She won't like your cave."

"I'll decorate it," promised Waldo. "I'll put in a proper kitchen."

"Suit yourself," shrugged Hetty, picking up her rock. "But personally, I reckon you're not her type. Too big. Too hairy. Not romantic enough."

"I don't care," said Waldo stubbornly. "Opposites attracts. I love her. And I *am* romantic. You'll see."

And he went back to his cave to write a poem.

The next morning he showed it to Hetty.
He waited impatiently while she finished her
push-ups, then thrust it under her nose.

Hetty read it as she towelled down. It was decorated with little hearts, and read:

Roses are red, daisies are white,
Princess Clarissa's a bit of all right.

"Well! What d'you think?" asked Waldo anxiously. "Is it meaningful? Does it get over what I'm trying to say? I've been working on it all night."

"It's OK," growled Hetty, thumping her punchbag.

"Really? Then I'll post it off straight away. I'm sure to get a reply soon."

13

But he didn't. A whole week went by, and there was no reply from the palace.

"It must have got lost in the post," Waldo told Hetty, who was breaking rocks. "So I've sent her a box of chocolates instead," he added. "I put a message inside. I put *From Your Biggest Admirer.* She sure to get those because they went by recorded delivery.

I expect she'll send me a perfumed thank-you note and invite me to tea by candlelight. I say, mind out, Het! That club came a bit too close to my foot for comfort."

He was wrong. Although the chocolates went by recorded delivery, there was still no word from Clarissa.

When another whole week had gone by, Waldo was desperate. He had run out of trees to carve *W luvs PC* on. Clarissa's picture had fallen to pieces as a result of so much anxious folding and unfolding.

He went to find Hetty, who was out jogging up the mountain.

"I can't understand it," he panted mournfully, struggling to keep up. "She must know how much I feel about her. Why doesn't she reply? I'm running out of romantic ideas."

"Flowers?" suggested Hetty, leaping a small precipice. "I've heard even stunted girls like flowers."

18

"Good idea!" cried Waldo joyfully. "I'll pick her a bunch right now. And then I shall go down to the palace and deliver it myself. That way I'll know she gets it. And — oh! Maybe I'll get to see her. Speak to her, even!"

Hetty watched him go crashing off down the slope. She gave a little sigh, then began to work on her pectorals.

Much, much later that day, aching slightly from an hour of sheep juggling, she was drinking cocoa in her cave when there came a knocking at the front boulder. Hetty rolled it aside, and there stood Waldo.

"Oh, it's you," said Hetty. "Well? Did she like the flowers?"

"I don't know," confessed Waldo, shaking his head sadly. "I didn't get beyond the front gate. The place was awash with soldiers for some reason. I asked the Captain of the Guard to give them to her, but I don't know if he did. He was very curt.

22

I waited around for ages, but she didn't come out and say thank you."

"I'd give up," advised Hetty.

"Give up? Never! Why, that girl gives me a spring in my step and a song in my heart!"

"Sing to her, then," snapped Hetty. "Go down there now and sing in the moonlight. Serenade her under her balcony. But don't expect me to wait up."

"Het," said Waldo. "Het, you're a genius."

And for the second time that day, he went crashing off down the mountain, pausing only to call into his cave to collect his guitar.

An hour or so later, he was back again.

"What happened?" asked Hetty, who *had* waited up. "Did you sing?"

"Yes," said Walso. "I sang. I sang 'Ten
Green Bottles'. It's the only one I know
from start to finish."

25

"Well? Did she come out? Not that I'm interested."

"Yes," sighed Waldo. "She came out. And so did her mum and dad and the Captain of the Guard."

"And what did they say?"

"They told me to clear off," admitted Waldo.

"They said I was a thundering great pest.
But, you know what, Het? I didn't care.
That Clarissa's nothing like her picture.
Up close, her nose is horrible. And she's got
this squeaky little voice. And you were right.

28

She only comes up to my knee. Much, much too small."

"I told you that to begin with," said Hetty.

"I know," said Waldo sheepishly. Then:

29

"Doing anything tomorrow night, Het?" he asked.

"Working out," said Hetty.

"Mind if I join you?" asked Waldo. "I'll bring my own weights. We could do a bit of arm-wrestling, maybe. By candlelight."

"Oh, Waldo," said Hetty, with a little blush. "You're so romantic."

Kaye Umansky is the enormously popular author of the "Pongwiffy" books, which were recently animated on television, with Jennifer Saunders and Dawn French as the main witches.

Like many writers Kaye is a former teacher, she lives in North London with her husband and daughter and her two cats Alfie and Charlie, who seem to think they help with the writing but in fact get in the way. In addition to writing wildly entertaining stories, Kaye also writes songs, plays and poems and is a very sought after speaker for schools.

SOME SIMILAR TITLES FROM

Barn Owl Books

ARABEL, MORTIMER AND THE ESCAPED BLACK MAMBA

Joan Tate and Quentin Blake

When Mortimer and Arabel are left with a babysitter all kinds of trouble result

ARABEL'S RAVEN

Joan Tate and Quentin Blake

Mortimer the raven finds the Joneses and causes chaos in Rumbury Town

MORTIMER'S BREAD BIN

Joan Tate and Quentin Blake

Mortimer wants to sleep in the bread bin but Mrs Jones thinks not

THE SPIRAL STAIR

Joan Tate and Quentin Blake

Giraffe thieves are about! Arabel and her raven have to act fast

THE BOY WHO SPROUTED ANTLERS

John Yeoman and Quentin Blake

When Billy says he can sprout antlers he doesn't really expect it to happen

JIMMY JELLY

Jacqueline Wilson and Lucy Keijser

A T.V. personality is confronted by his greatest fan